For Betty Connors and Travis Bogard
with gratitude and admiration
J.G.

For Stella with thanks
A.H.

Text copyright © 1995 by Judith Gorog
Illustrations copyright © 1995 by Amanda Harvey

First edition 1995

Library of Congress Cataloging-in-Publication Data

Gorog, Judith.
Zilla Sasparilla and the mud baby / Judith Gorog ;
illustrated by Amanda Harvey.— 1st ed.

Summary: After she pulls a baby from the mud, Zilla takes care of
him and watches him grow, all the while worrying that she will lose
him back to the Little Muddy River.
ISBN 1-56402-295-1 (alk. paper)
[1. Fairy tales. 2. Mother and child—Fiction.]
I. Harvey, Amanda, ill. II. Title.
PZ8.G665Zi   1995
[E]—dc20   95-16163

10 9 8 7 6 5 4 3 2 1

Printed in Italy

This book was typeset in Columbus MT.
The pictures were done in watercolor and pencil.

Candlewick Press
2067 Massachusetts Avenue
Cambridge, Massachusetts 02140

Zilla Sasparilla

-«- and the -»-
Mud Baby

JUDITH GOROG   *illustrated by* **AMANDA HARVEY**

CANDLEWICK PRESS
CAMBRIDGE, MASSACHUSETTS

The way home was a path through the deep woods. That path, all slippery after a solid week of rain, ran alongside Little Muddy River. Zilla put one of her big feet down on a clump of weeds, the other on the driest tuft of grass she could see. She went slowly, trying to keep her shoes out of the sloppy mud.

Once, she peeked at the thin red line where the sun had gone down. Maybe tomorrow would be clear.

"You there. Little Muddy River. Hear me," Zilla insisted. "You don't need more rain, you wicked old river. You don't need to rear up over your banks!"

Lecturing that way, Zilla forgot to watch the path. With a great sucking sound, her left foot disappeared into the muck. Zilla yanked back hard and fell on her bottom. Both feet went into the air, the rest of her very much into the mud.

Zilla stood up, gave her skirt a long sad look, then noticed how cold the ground felt to her naked left foot. Her shoe had disappeared and Zilla wanted it back. She knelt down, took a deep breath, then plunged into the mud with both hands. Clear to her elbows Zilla reached before she felt that shoe. She pulled. The shoe did not budge.

"Oh, no you don't," Zilla told the mud. With tremendous effort, she hauled at the shoe, fell backward with a *thwack*, but cried "Aha!" all the same.

She sat right up to look at her muddy hands, thinking that in those hands she would see her left shoe.

Oh my. Sure enough, Zilla's shoe was there, but holding on to the shoe, with both plump fists, was a slithery mud-golden baby, the most beautiful mud baby in the world.

Zilla wrapped the mud baby in her shawl and cradled him in her arms, singing and coaxing all the while. At last, he let go of her shoe and reached up to touch her face.

Holding that mud baby in her arms, Zilla struggled into her shoe, and started on the long way home. All the while she sang, "Oh my goodness. You wonderful baby. Oh, how I'll raise you."

The mud baby smiled up at her. He gurgled. Surely he agreed.

"And then," Zilla told him, "when I am very old, you'll be a good son and read to me when I can't see." At this the mud baby chortled. Zilla hugged him once more just to feel that he was real.

Out of the dark woods, away from the river, Zilla walked toward home. Every house had lamps already lit; tables were set for supper. As she approached, doors opened and out came her friends, calling, "Zilla. Zilla. How'd you get so muddy? And is that a genuine mud baby in your arms?"

Zilla told. All her friends sighed in admiration. And every time she finished her telling, someone would ask, "And Zilla, did you get your shoe?"

At last Zilla waved good-bye. For all her singing and telling, she was troubled, so she walked right past her own house and up the hill to a little place set off by itself.

With the night all dark around her, she trudged up the wooden steps and rapped at the door. "Granny. Granny Vi," she called. "It's Zilla Sasparilla come to ask you a question."

"Door's open!" a voice called. "Come on in, Zilla!"

"Can't. I'm all over with mud."

"Little mud never hurt anyone," said the old woman who opened the door. "Why, Zilla, is that a mud baby?"

"Yes ma'am, and I'm so worried. What if the heat from my stove dries him all out so that in the morning he won't be a baby at all?" Zilla whispered, covering the baby's ears with her hands. "What if this sweet little baby cracks like an old mud vase?"

"No. No. No. Child, dry your tears. My granny told me that mud babies have to be washed first in milk and then in water. Afterward, heat won't hurt them a particle, not more than it will any human baby, because that's what he'll be. Then, tomorrow, you take him straight to church and have him named. After he's been washed and named, don't you ever call him mud baby again. If others do, it doesn't matter. Understand?"

Zilla nodded. "Yessum."

"So go on home now. Looks like you both need a bath."

Zilla had plenty to do, with a fire to make and milk and water to heat and sewing an old undershirt to make the baby a gown. Zilla washed him—first in milk and then in water to keep him safe. Then she fed that hungry baby and tucked a blanket around him and put him into her dresser drawer. He sighed once and slept.

Then Zilla really set to work. She brushed the mud from her skirt and washed her shawl and hung it to dry. She scraped and brushed every bit of mud from her shoes, then polished them. She swept her house, gave herself a bath, and brushed her hair. Then, at last, warm in her nightgown and robe, Zilla sat down to eat her supper.

The next morning, Zilla had the baby fed and dressed and her own hat on her head before she found time to drink a cup of coffee. She thought they'd be the first ones at church, but when she stepped out onto her porch, all her friends were coming along the path. They brought her this and that, soft clean clothes their own babies had outgrown, a rattle, a dolly, a book full of bright colors.

Zilla was proud of the baby in church. He smiled and looked around but never cried once, no matter how many people fussed over him. When the time came for her to call out his name, Zilla's voice cracked. "I thought . . ." She hesitated. "I thought to name him Cinnamon because he is the color of a beautiful piece of cinnamon toast, but maybe that's not got dignity enough."

"Cinnamon's a fine name!" someone called. "Got a bit of spice to it. The boy's got spunk—you see!" Indeed Cinnamon fairly stood up in Zilla's arms, gurgling and cooing at the sunbeams pouring through the church windows.

Cinnamon it was. Of course, the news spread. Everyone in the country knew how Zilla Sasparilla had pulled up a mud baby when she'd rescued her shoe. For a week, the path beside the Little Muddy River was crowded with people trying to find a mud baby for themselves. No one did, even though old Mrs. Willis plopped her right shoe and her left shoe and her pocketbook deep into the mud and never got a thing back.

Singing, Zilla carried Cinnamon to work in the morning and home again in the evening. She fed him and changed him, bathed him and dried him. She told him rhymes on his fingers and on his toes. She hugged him and kissed him, so glad that he was real.

After a time, Cinnamon learned to walk beside Zilla, holding on to her finger. From walking he went to running and playing, and the next thing, Zilla was worrying. First, she worried a little and then a lot. Finally, late one night, she went knocking at Granny Vi's door.

Granny Vi squinted up at Zilla, said, "Shusshhh," and took the heavy sleeping Cinnamon out of her arms and put him on the bed. Granny Vi made Zilla sit down, drink a cup of coffee, and eat a piece of lemon pie before she'd let Zilla say a word. At last, Granny Vi looked up from her mending. "Zilla. I notice you are worrying."

Zilla tiptoed over to put her hands over Cinnamon's ears while she told. "*Ohhh*. After I bathe him . . . the water—It's *sooo* muddy. What ever will I do if I wash him away?"

"Zilla. How many children have you washed?" demanded Granny Vi.

"Oh, I don't know. Lots."

"And what color was the water when you finished washing the children?"

"Muddy?"

"Yes," said Granny. "And wasn't there always plenty of child left? Here's a big hug for you. Go home and get some sleep."

Zilla went home, singing.

Afterward, for a good long while, Zilla sang and Cinnamon grew, until he went to school with the other children. At first, Zilla liked to watch him leave with his books and his lunch.

But Cinnamon kept on growing, and the bigger he got, the farther he went from home. Zilla told him to stay away from the river, but Cinnamon forgot.

When he was out of sight, Zilla worried that Little Muddy River wanted to steal Cinnamon and take him into the deep dark mud.

To keep Cinnamon safe, Zilla made a plan to move far away from Little Muddy River. Without telling a soul, she bought a mule and wagon. That same day, while Cinnamon was in school, she loaded everything they owned onto that wagon, so that it shook in a towering heap.

Cinnamon came home to find Zilla in front of their empty house. She handed him an apple, saying, "Come on, now. Help me lead this mule."

Cinnamon walked alongside Zilla and the mule. "But why?"

"It's the only wagon road to get you away from this river," said Zilla.

Cinnamon started to ask more, but Zilla pulled on the mule, saying, "Hush. I'll tell you when it's safe."

As soon as they got to the muddy path alongside the river, the mule locked its knees and would not budge.

"See!" cried Zilla. "Even this old mule hates that river." Zilla ran around the wagon to push, calling to Cinnamon that he should pull the mule ahead. Cinnamon coaxed. Zilla pushed with all her might. The wagon stood still, but Zilla's two big feet slipped right out from under her. *Whoosh.* Zilla slid off the path and straight into the river. Down she went, underwater. Up she came, sputtering. Her hat went in one direction, her shawl in another. Her clothes were heavy with muddy water.

But worst of all, Cinnamon let go of the mule and dived into the river!

"No!" cried Zilla, but only once. There was Cinnamon, up and down and all around, splashing and laughing, swimming in the river. He helped Zilla clamber up the slippery bank. After that, he swam out to rescue her hat and shawl; though her two big shoes were not to be found.

"Ohhh," warned Zilla, "you mustn't swim alone."

"I didn't." Cinnamon grinned. "You're here."

Zilla sat on the bank—mud from head to toe. Cinnamon and the mule turned the wagon around so they could go back home.

When they got there, Zilla unpacked the wagon and set the house in order. Cinnamon gave the mule food and water, a good rub down, and a name.

Before the weather got cold, Cinnamon and the mule earned enough money to buy Zilla a new pair of shoes.

And, if she has not lost them, Zilla is wearing them still.